My Family Celebrates
CHRISTMAS

Lisa Bullard

Illustrated by **Katie Saunders**

LERNER PUBLICATIONS◆MINNEAP

NOTE TO EDUCATORS

Find text recall questions at the end of each chapter. Critical-thinking and text feature questions are available on page 23. These help young readers learn to think critically about the topic by using the text, text features, and illustrations.

Lerner Publications Company
A division of Lerner Publishing Group, Inc.
241 First Avenue North
Minneapolis, MN 55401 USA

For reading levels and more information, look up this title at www.lernerbooks.com.

Photos on p. 22 used with permission of: Smileus/Shutterstock.com (Christmas tree); SKPG_Arts/Shutterstock.com (cookies); Milles Studio/Shutterstock.com (Santa).

Main body text set in Billy Infant 22/28.
Typeface provided by SparkyType.

Library of Congress Cataloging-in-Publication Data

Names: Bullard, Lisa, author. | Saunders, Katie, illustrator.
Title: My family celebrates Christmas / Lisa Bullard ; illustrated by Katie Saunders.
Description: Minneapolis : Lerner Publications, 2019. | Series: Holiday time (Early bird stories) | Includes bibliographical references and index. | Audience: Age 5–8. | Audience: K to grade 3.
Identifiers: LCCN 2017049346 (print) | LCCN 2017056390 (ebook) | ISBN 9781541524965 (eb pdf) | ISBN 9781541520073 (lb : alk. paper) | ISBN 9781541527386 (pb : alk. paper)
Subjects: LCSH: Christmas—Juvenile literature.
Classification: LCC GT4985.5 (ebook) | LCC GT4985.5 .B864 2019 (print) | DDC 394.2663—dc23

LC record available at https://lccn.loc.gov/2017049346

Manufactured in the United States of America
1-44343-34589-12/27/2017

TABLE OF CONTENTS

Chapter 1
Christmas Is Coming.....4

Chapter 2
Christmas Tastes Great.....10

Chapter 3
The Christmas Story.....12

Chapter 4
Present Time!.....18

Learn about Holidays....22

Think about Holidays:
Critical-Thinking and Text Feature Questions....23

Glossary....24

To Learn More....24

Index....24

CHRISTMAS IS COMING

Ho, ho, ho!

My name is Carter. I'm making an ornament for my grandma.

4

It's her Christmas present, and I'm trying
to keep it a secret.

Carter Xmas
list ..
B~~i~~ke, scooter
Sneakers.
football game

It's time to go Christmas shopping. We need to find gifts for everyone on our list.

LINE STARTS **HERE**

I get to see Santa Claus
at the mall too!

On the way home, we stop to buy our Christmas tree.
Grandma asks me to help her decorate it right away.

But when will I work on her present?

**Why does Carter
go shopping?**

CHRISTMAS TASTES GREAT

It's Christmas Eve. I'm still not done with the ornament. But I can't work on it now!

We're decorating cookies with our neighbors. The cookies are shaped like things that make us think of Christmas.

Who decorates cookies with Carter?

THE CHRISTMAS STORY

We go to church that night and sing carols.

The pastor tells the Christmas story.
It's about Jesus being born long ago.
That's what my family celebrates at Christmas.

Jesus's mother was Mary.
She was engaged to marry Joseph.
They were traveling when Jesus was born.

They didn't have a bed for Jesus.
He had to sleep in a manger!
That's a box that holds animal food.

After church, we drive by houses decorated with lights.

Where does Jesus sleep when he's born?

17

CHAPTER 4

PRESENT TIME!

Finally, Grandma goes to bed. I sneak out to the kitchen to finish that ornament!

cookies

I listen for Santa while I work. I hope he
doesn't mind that I'm eating his cookies.

Lots of relatives come over on Christmas.
We eat tasty food and open presents.

Who does Carter listen for when he works on Grandma's ornament?

But Grandma says that she got the best present of all!

LEARN ABOUT HOLIDAYS

A man called Saint Nicholas lived 1,700 years ago. He loved to give gifts. Over time, Saint Nicholas became known as Santa Claus in many places.

Jesus was born about two thousand years ago. Some people believe Jesus is the son of God. These people are called Christians.

In Germany, evergreen trees are a Christmas tradition. Germans who moved to the United States brought the tradition with them.

Different things stand for Christmas in different places. In India, people decorate banana trees instead of evergreens. In Australia, some people picture kangaroos pulling Santa's sleigh.

Many people around the world celebrate Christmas on December 25.

THINK ABOUT HOLIDAYS:
CRITICAL-THINKING AND TEXT FEATURE QUESTIONS

Why does Carter's family celebrate Christmas?

Does your family do special things to celebrate a winter holiday?

How many chapters are in this book?

Where can you find page numbers in this book?

Expand learning beyond the printed book. Download free, complementary educational resources for this book from our website, www.lerneresource.com.

GLOSSARY

carol: a song about Christmas

decorate: to add things to something to make it look pretty

manger: an open box where food for animals such as horses or cows is placed

ornament: a thing that decorates something else. Ornaments are small items that hang from the branches of Christmas trees.

pastor: a person who leads a church

relative: a family member

TO LEARN MORE

BOOKS

Schuh, Mari. *Crayola Christmas Colors.* Minneapolis: Lerner Publications, 2019. Celebrate the spirit and colors of Christmas in this book.

Wallace, Adam. *How to Catch an Elf.* Naperville, IL: Sourcebooks Jabberwocky, 2016. This funny picture book follows a clever elf as he avoids being caught by children.

WEBSITE

Christmas Around the World
https://www.whychristmas.com/cultures/
Learn how Christmas is celebrated in countries around the world on this fun website.

INDEX

Christmas tree, 8
cookies, 11, 19

Jesus, 13–15, 17

ornament, 4, 10, 18, 20

present, 5, 9, 18, 20–21

Santa Claus, 7, 19